DEMCO

HENRY'S
SHOW AND TELL

by Nancy Carlson

To all my kindergarten friends!

VIKING
Published by Penguin Group
Penguin Young Readers Group
345 Hudson Street, New York, New York 10014, U.S.A.
Penguin Books Ltd, 80 Strand, London WC2R 0RL, England
Penguin Books Australia Ltd, 250 Camberwell Road, Camberwell, Victoria 3124, Australia
Penguin Books Canada Ltd, 10 Alcorn Avenue, Toronto, Ontario, Canada M4V 3B2
Penguin Books (N.Z.) Ltd, 182-190 Wairau Road, Auckland 10, New Zealand

Published in 2004 by Viking, a division of Penguin Young Readers Group.

1 3 5 7 9 10 8 6 4 2

Copyright © Nancy Carlson, 2004

LIBRARY OF CONGRESS CATALOGING-IN-PUBLICATION DATA
Carlson, Nancy.
Henry's show and tell / by Nancy Carlson.
p. cm.
Summary: Henry likes everything about kindergarten except show-and-tell, but with
the help of his teacher and his pet lizard he is able to overcome his fear.
ISBN 0-670-03695-1 (HARDCOVER)
[1. Show-and-tell presentations—Fiction. 2. Kindergarten—Fiction.
3. Schools—Fiction.] I. Title.
PZ7.C21665He 2004
[E—dc22
2003019481

Manufactured in China
Set in Avenir
Book designed by Kelley McIntyre

Henry really liked kindergarten.

He liked listening to stories,

learning his letters,

singing songs,

and painting pictures.

Henry liked playing games outside

and getting great big hugs from his teacher,
Ms. Bradley.

But there was one thing about kindergarten

that Henry did not like. . . . Show and tell!

During show and tell, kids shared facts about their pets,

their interesting collections,

and what they did on vacation.

But whenever Henry tried to share, he felt all shaky.

"Why don't you wait until next time to share?"
said Ms. Bradley.

But next time, Henry still felt too shy to speak.

Everyone else could share.
Tony brought his baseball cards.

Vinney told all about his trip to Wisconsin.

Even shy little Kathryn with the quiet voice told about her snow globe.

But Henry still couldn't speak when it was his turn.
"Is he going to barf?" asked Tony.

That day, before recess, Ms. Bradley had
an idea for Henry.

"Bring something that's fun for you to talk about.
Then practice in the mirror, and you'll do just fine,"
said Ms. Bradley.

Henry decided to tell about his lizard, Wallace.

He even practiced in front of his little brother Pete.

"I'm ready for show and tell!" thought Henry.

The next day when it was Henry's turn, he walked to the front of the class. Just when he was about to share . . .

Wallace escaped!

By the time Henry finally caught Wallace

he forgot all about being shy, and
he told everyone all about lizards.

"Good job!" said Ms. Bradley
"That was cool," said Tony.

The next week when it was Henry's turn to share, he just stood there.

"Henry looks sick again!" said Tony.
"Are you nervous?" whispered Ms. Bradley.

"I'm not nervous!" said Henry.
"It's just that I have nothing to share because . . ."

"My pet spider got loose!"
"Recess!" said Ms. Bradley.